Thea
the Thursday Fairy

by Daisy Meadows

SCHOLASTIC INC.

New York   Toronto   London   Auckland   Sydney
Mexico City   New Delhi   Hong Kong   Buenos Aires

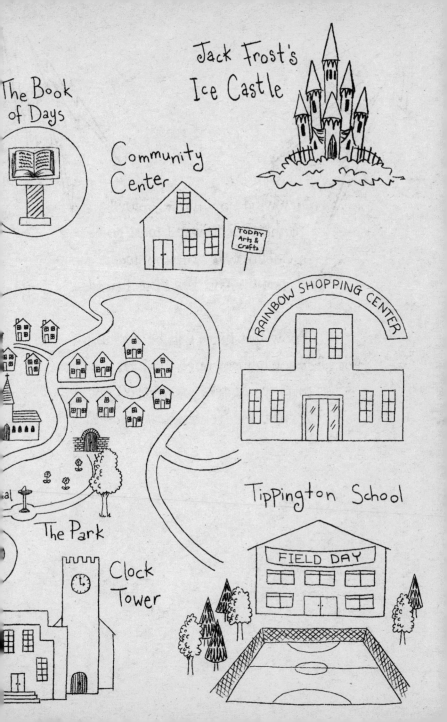

Icy wind now fiercely blow!
To the Time Tower I must go.
Goblins will all follow me
And steal the Fun Day Flags I need.

I know that there will be no fun,
For fairies or humans once the flags are gone.
Storm winds, take me where I say.
My plan for trouble starts today!

Contents

Spectacular Seahorses

"A tropical reef, a sunken ship, sea otters, seahorses, giant Japanese spider crabs, reef sharks . . .wow!" Rachel Walker looked up from the colorful brochure she was holding and grinned at her friend, Kirsty Tate. "We're going to have a fabulous time here!"

The two girls had come to the Morristown Aquarium for the day with Rachel's parents. Kirsty was spending the week of school vacation with Rachel, and they had been having a very exciting time. A very magical time, too!

"We'll meet you back here at four o'clock," Mrs. Walker said, as they all strolled into the lobby. "Have fun!"

"We will," Rachel said cheerfully. Then she gazed at some of the other people nearby. "Although it doesn't look as if anyone else is having much fun," she whispered to Kirsty.

Kirsty looked around. Rachel was right. There were plenty of visitors at the aquarium, but they didn't seem to be enjoying themselves.

"I don't even like fish," they heard one boy mutter. "Why did we have to come here?"

Rachel and Kirsty gave each other a knowing look as Rachel's parents wandered off to look at the first exhibit.

They knew exactly why the mood at the aquarium was so glum. It was because the Thursday Fun Day Flag was missing!

Rachel and Kirsty were friends with the fairies. All week, the two girls had been busy helping the fairies solve a big problem. Nasty Jack Frost had stolen the seven Fun Day Flags from the Time Tower in Fairyland. Without the flags, the Fun Day Fairies couldn't spread their special magic around the human world. Jack Frost had taken the flags back to his castle, but he soon decided that this was a mistake: his goblins were having so much fun, they had stopped doing any work! In a rage, Jack Frost had thrown the flags into the human world, and now Rachel and Kirsty were helping the

fairies find them. But Jack Frost didn't know that the sneaky goblins were trying to get the flags back, too!

Kirsty turned to Rachel. "We've just got to find that Thursday flag before the goblins do," she whispered. "We really need to cheer everybody up in here."

"Definitely," Rachel agreed. "But you know what the fairies say — we have to let the magic find us. So why don't we look at some of the exhibits?" She opened the map inside her brochure, and Kirsty leaned over for a closer look.

"Ooh, seahorses, I love those," Kirsty said, pointing to a picture.

"Let's head for the tropical reef exhibit, then," Rachel suggested. "That's where all the seahorses are."

The girls walked along a long hallway lined with fish tanks. They stopped to see the large orange-and-purple angel fish elegantly gliding along, the yellow-and-white butterfly fish darting here and there, and the bright orange-and-white clown fish swimming in playful circles.

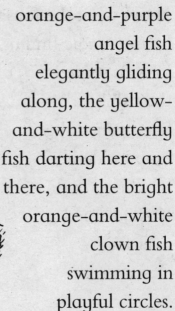

"And here are the seahorses!" Rachel said, as they stopped in front of the next tank.

Kirsty and Rachel both peered through the glass to watch the beautiful red-and-yellow creatures bobbing up and down like tiny dragons. There were rocks and coral at the bottom of their tanks, and long green weeds, which the seahorses seemed to like hiding behind.

"Wow!" Kirsty exclaimed. "That one just changed color, from yellow to black!"

"Amazing!" Rachel commented, studying the information plaque. "Yeah, this says that these seahorses can turn from black or gray to yellow or red. How cool!"

"Oh, and look — baby seahorses!" Kirsty cooed. "They're so adorable. Can you see them?" Suddenly, Kirsty heard a friendly voice behind her say, "Ahh, but did you know that with seahorses it's the dad who has the babies, not the mom?"

The girls turned to see a member of the aquarium staff smiling at them.

"Really?" Rachel asked, interested. "I didn't know that."

The guide started telling the girls about how the female seahorses fought over the male seahorses with the biggest bellies! "That's where the males have their breeding pouch," he explained. "So, the bigger the belly, the better the father — but that only counts for seahorses!"

Rachel laughed, and Kirsty nodded, but Rachel could tell that her friend was kind of distracted. She was staring into the tank, and it was only when the guide walked away again that Kirsty turned to Rachel, her eyes shining.

"Look who it is!" she whispered, pointing at the glass.

Rachel followed the line of Kirsty's finger and a smile lit up her face. At the back of the tank, riding a yellow seahorse with blue spots, sat a tiny smiling fairy, and she was waving right at the girls!

Underwater Fairy

"It's Thea the Thursday Fairy!" Rachel said, her voice hushed with excitement. "Hello again, Thea!" The girls had met all seven of the Fun Day Fairies when they'd been magically whisked to Fairyland on Monday.

Thea guided her seahorse toward the girls with a grin. She had long golden

hair, and she wore a long-sleeved lilac
dress with a white belt. A beautiful
necklace with an amethyst pendant
sparkled at her throat.

Thea's seahorse floated right up to the
glass, and Thea started to say something
to the girls, pointing behind them.
Unfortunately, the tank's glass was so
thick, Rachel and Kirsty couldn't hear
what she was saying.

"What's she pointing at?" Kirsty wondered aloud, turning to see. "Ah! Do you think she means we should meet her over there?"

Rachel looked where Kirsty had motioned. A large seahorse sculpture stood in the corner of the room near a tank of silver eels. When she turned back to the glass, she saw that Thea was nodding enthusiastically at them.

"I think so," Rachel said, smiling. "Okay, Thea, we'll see you there in a minute!"

The two girls went over to the
sculpture at once, both feeling excited

that another fairy
adventure was
about to begin.
"I'm looking
forward to hearing the
next poem from the
Book of Days," Kirsty
said in a low voice.

"Me, too," Rachel said. "Hopefully it
will give us a clue about where the
missing flag is. It might even be in one of
the tanks!"

The girls grinned at each other. The
Book of Days was like no other book.
Francis, Fairyland's Royal Time Guard,
used it to tell which day it was and
which flag he should fly on the royal

flagpole every morning. But ever since the flags had been stolen, a new riddle had magically appeared in the book each day. So far, the riddles had helped Rachel, Kirsty, and the fairies find three of the missing Fun Day Flags.

"Looking for the flags is like the best kind of treasure hunt," Kirsty said happily. "It's — "

But before Kirsty could finish her sentence, Rachel nudged her friend. "I just saw a goblin!" she squeaked. "Look — he's snorkeling with those eels!"

Kirsty and Rachel hid behind the

sculpture so that the goblin wouldn't notice them. He was swimming along at the top of the tank, wearing a snorkel mask and big flippers. Luckily, there was no one else in the room to spot him.

"He must think the Thursday flag is in there," Kirsty said in a low voice. "Can you see it anywhere, Rachel?"

The two friends looked cautiously into the tank, searching all around for a sparkly fairy flag, but there was no sign of it.

Just then, the air beside the sculpture shimmered, and Thea appeared in a flurry of pink sparkles.

"Hello again," Rachel said. Then she gazed curiously at the smiling fairy. "I thought you'd be wet after your swim, but you're completely dry!" she said with surprise.

"And you could breathe underwater, without a bubble helmet!" Kirsty added. "When we went underwater with Joy the Summer Vacation Fairy, we had to use magic bubbles. Why didn't you need one?"

Thea winked and twirled her wand between her fingers. "Fairy magic is wonderful stuff," she laughed.

"It's lucky you're here," Rachel went on, "because look who's in this eel tank!"

Thea turned and saw

the swimming goblin, but she didn't seem worried. "Don't worry," she assured the girls. "He won't find anything in there. I've already checked all the tanks in this area, and the Thursday Fun Flag definitely isn't in any of them."

"But it is in the aquarium?" Kirsty asked eagerly.

"Yes," Thea said, "but we're going to have to be really careful, because we're not the only ones looking for it. There are goblins all over the place!"

Goblins Galore!

Rachel and Kirsty looked around
nervously. They certainly didn't want
any of the lurking goblins to know that
they were searching for the Thursday
Fun Flag, too!

Once she was sure that they weren't
going to be overheard, Rachel turned
back to Thea. "Has a new poem

appeared in the Book of Days?" she asked.

Thea nodded. "Francis read it to me this morning," she replied. "This is how it goes." The fairy lowered her voice and recited:

"Seahorses, turtles, and sharks abound.
In the aquarium, the flag will be found.
Look among all the beautiful fish;
On the back of the whale, you'll find
*   your wish."*

"*On the back of the whale . . .*" Kirsty repeated thoughtfully. "Rachel, are there any whales in this aquarium?"

Rachel unfolded her brochure and scanned it quickly. "There's a whale shark exhibit nearby," she announced. "The flag might be there."

"Let's go and see!" Thea said, fluttering into Kirsty's pocket.

The whale sharks' tank was in the next room. After the small seahorse tanks, it seemed enormous, stretching across one whole wall.

"Look how humongous the whale

sharks are!" Rachel exclaimed. "No wonder they need such a big tank."

"These two are called Griffin and Chloe, and they're over twenty feet long," Kirsty said, reading the sign next to the tank. "Whale sharks are the biggest fish in the ocean. They can grow to be fifty feet long!" she added with a whistle.

Rachel peered in at the majestic whale sharks as they nosed their way around their tank. They were dark gray, with yellow dots and stripes on their bodies. Neither creature had a Fun Day Flag on its back. "Maybe the flag floated off and sank to the bottom of the tank," she suggested.

The three friends drew closer to the

tank for a better look. There was sand at
its base, with clumps of
brown seaweed and
piles of rocks here
and there. Schools
of colorful fish
darted around
the whale
sharks, not at all
bothered by the
size of their neighbors.

"Oh!" Thea gasped suddenly, from
where she was peeking out of Kirsty's
pocket. "Look!"

Kirsty peered into the tank, hoping
Thea had spotted her sparkly flag, but
she hadn't. What she had seen were two
scuba divers with masks on their faces

and oxygen tanks on their backs,
slithering along the bottom of the tank.
The divers had big green feet and long,
pointy noses.

"Oh, no!" Kirsty cried, as she realized
who they were.

"More goblins!" Rachel groaned.
"They beat us to it!"

"What have they found?" Kirsty asked in dismay, as she watched one of the goblin divers pull at something pink that was lodged between two rocks. He beckoned his friend over. The second goblin went to help, blocking the girls' view in the process.

Both goblins tugged eagerly at their find, and Thea's face fell.

"Oh no!" She gasped. "My flag is pink. I think they've got my Thursday Fun Flag!"

Flag Ahoy!

The girls and Thea held their breath as the goblins yanked on the pink thing. Finally, the rocks shifted and the first goblin held up his hand victoriously. But his look of triumph turned sour when he realized he was clutching a piece of pink seaweed. It wasn't the Thursday flag after all! His friend poked him angrily

and shook his head, which prompted the
first goblin to throw the clump of
seaweed in a huff. It was
obvious that neither
goblin was very
happy.

"Thank
goodness it was
only seaweed."
Thea breathed
a sigh of relief.

"Look! I think
Griffin and Chloe are coming to
introduce themselves to the
goblins," Kirsty said, her
eyes wide. Both whale
sharks seemed to have noticed
the disturbance, and now they

were swimming straight
toward the goblins!
The goblins suddenly
looked up to see the
huge faces of
Griffin and Chloe
looming in front
of them. With
a jump of
alarm, the
goblins began
swimming
away as fast as
they could. The
sharks followed,
curious.
"Oh no! The sharks
aren't going

to eat them, are they?" Kirsty cried anxiously.

Rachel laughed. "No," she said, pointing at the information board in front of her. "It says here that whale sharks are filter feeders who strain their food through their gills." She grinned. "They're not dangerous at all — their food has to be tiny to fit through their gills. They couldn't eat the goblins even if they wanted to!"

Thea couldn't help giggling at the frantic goblins. "Something tells me that the goblins don't know that," she laughed.

"It doesn't look like the flag is in there, anyway," Kirsty added, smiling as the goblins floundered toward the top of the tank. "Are there any other whales in the aquarium guide, Rachel?"

Rachel consulted her brochure again. "Yes," she said. "There's a beluga whale exhibit in the aquarium. We have to go through the underwater tunnel to get there. This way!"

Rachel led them out of the room and into a huge, brightly lit tunnel, where crowds of people were gazing all around. The sides and roof of the tunnel were made of thick glass, and the girls slowed down, staring in wonder at the schools of

brightly colored fish, sting rays, and turtles swimming right over their heads. A big green turtle came up to the glass near Kirsty and seemed to give her a friendly wink. She waved and smiled at him through the tunnel wall.

"We'd better go and find the beluga whales," she said after a few minutes. She was reluctant to leave the tunnel, but she knew that finding the flag was more important. "We can always come back here later. . . ."

Just then, Rachel gasped. Kirsty looked around to see that her friend was pointing at something in the tank farther down the tunnel. It was the sunken wreck of a pirate ship, with fish swimming in and out of it. As Kirsty drew closer, she saw that the name on the side of the ship's hull was . . . *The Whale!*

"This might be the whale we're looking for!" Kirsty murmured excitedly. "Good eye, Rachel!"

"Yes, and look what's on the mast," Rachel whispered joyfully. "Thea's flag!"

Kirsty and Thea gazed up at the ship's sails to see that Rachel was right. Waving gently in the water at the top of the mast was the Thursday Fun Flag! It was a beautiful dusty pink color, with a large glittery sun on it.

"We found it," Thea declared happily. "Wonderful!"

Kirsty gave Rachel a nudge. "But look who else is about to find it, too," she whispered in dismay.

Rachel and Thea turned to see three goblins dressed as little boys tromping through the tunnel.

"Oh no!" Thea said in an anguished whisper. "We can't let them see the flag!"

Goblin Danger

A smile suddenly lit up Kirsty's face. "I have had an idea," she said in a low voice. "Don't look at the ship, OK?"

Rachel nodded and turned to look at a strange sand-colored fish that was rising slowly through the water. "OK," she whispered.

"I figured it out!" Kirsty said to

Rachel in a loud voice, pretending that she hadn't noticed the goblins nearby. "I know exactly where the Thursday Fun Flag must be!"

From the corner of her eye, Rachel saw the three goblins slow down to eavesdrop on Kirsty. She grinned and began playing along with her clever friend. "Oh, where is it?" she asked eagerly.

"Well, the poem said it was on the back of a whale, didn't it?" Kirsty went on. "And the beluga whale exhibit is at the end of this tunnel!"

The goblins immediately rushed away. They ran down the tunnel, giggling with glee — and completely missed seeing the pirate ship with its Fun Day Flag treasure!

Thea fluttered out of Kirsty's pocket, smiling. "Your plan worked!" she cried happily.

Kirsty was smiling, too. "Hopefully that will keep those goblins

safely out of the way, while we get the flag!"

Just then, an announcement came over the intercom system. "We will be feeding the sea otters in five minutes," a voice said. "Please make your way to the otter exhibit now, if you would like to watch." The other visitors in the tunnel started drifting away to see the otters.

"Perfect," Thea whispered, hiding behind Kirsty's hair. "Now the coast is clear for some flag-collecting!"

She waved her wand over the girls, and

a stream of pink sparkles showered down
on them. Rachel and Kirsty felt
themselves shrinking until they were the
same size as Thea. They smiled when
they saw the sparkling wings on their
backs. They were fairies again!

"Since we need to get into the tank,
I've given you some underwater magic,
too," Thea said. "Then you'll still be
able to breathe when we're in the
water."

"How do we get in?" Rachel asked, fluttering her wings with excitement.

Thea was already flying ahead to a door marked STAFF ONLY at the end of  the tunnel. "This way," she called. Kirsty, Rachel, and Thea slipped through the gap under the door. On the other side, they saw tall ladders that stretched to the top of the tank. Kirsty guessed the ladders were for feeding. The tank was open at the top, so the three fairies flew up and over the side.

Splash! Splash! Splash! The friends plunged into the water, which was nice and warm.

"Now that I can breathe underwater, I feel just like a mermaid," Rachel said happily, as they swam down toward the ship. A whole school of silvery fish came over and gave them curious looks. "Hello," Kirsty said in a friendly way as she passed. "We're just dropping by to get something. Don't worry."

"There it is," Rachel said, as they neared the ship.

Kirsty joined her and, together, the girls carefully unhooked the shimmering flag

from the top of the mast. Then they swam over to Thea, towing the flag behind them.

"Thank you," Thea said happily. She touched her wand to the Thursday flag, and it shrank down to its Fairyland size. Then she waved her wand again and a flurry of twinkling pink lights danced through the water toward the ship. Within seconds, a new flag was attached

to the mast. This flag had a slightly
different pink-and-silver design.

"We did it!" Kirsty cheered. "Let's get
out of here!"

But even as her friend spoke, Rachel
cried out in alarm. Four goblin divers
had emerged from inside the shipwreck!

One of the goblins spotted the flag in
Thea's hand and pointed at it furiously.
He quickly swam toward the girls,
followed by his three friends.

"Quick!" Rachel called, as she, Kirsty,
and Thea began swimming away as fast
as they could. But they were so tiny that
it wasn't long before the goblins were
closing in on them. Rachel could see that
it would only be a few seconds before
they were surrounded — and trapped!

Turtle Power

Kirsty was getting tired when she saw the turtle she'd waved to earlier swim by. The turtle zoomed right up to Thea. He seemed to be saying something.

"Oh, thank you," Thea replied after a moment, looking relieved. "He asked if we would like a ride," she told the girls.

"Yes, please!" Kirsty and Rachel accepted gratefully. They scrambled onto the turtle's smooth green shell, as the goblins drew closer. Thea climbed aboard, too, and the turtle immediately kicked his powerful flippers. The group was soon shooting through the water with great speed. Within seconds, they had left the goblins far behind.

The turtle looked over his shoulder, his kindly eyes twinkling. Thea grinned. "He just told me he's going to take the goblins on a little tour," she explained to Kirsty and Rachel.

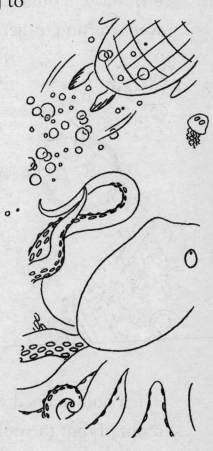

Rachel smiled as the space between them and the goblins grew. The turtle zoomed along on a zig-zag route around some rocks, over some bright red coral, and past a large, surprised-looking octopus.

"They're still chasing us," Kirsty said, looking around to check.

But it was quite clear that the goblins were starting to get tired now. One of  them had already given up. He was slumped over a rock, watching the others. The remaining three goblins were slowing down, too. They seemed to be arguing about whose fault it was that the girls and Thea had escaped with the flag. Kirsty realized that the goblins would never be able to catch up with them now, and she

gave a sigh of relief. The turtle swam
smoothly up to the surface of the tank,
and Kirsty, Rachel, and Thea slipped off
his back.

"Thank you so much," Thea
said to him.

"Yes, thank you,"
Rachel added.
"You saved
us — and the
Thursday flag."

"Good-bye,"
Kirsty said,
giving the turtle a
gentle pat.

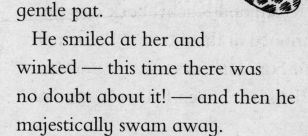

He smiled at her and
winked — this time there was
no doubt about it! — and then he
majestically swam away.

Kirsty, Rachel, and Thea climbed out of the tank, shaking their heavy, wet wings behind them. Thea waved her wand and, instantly, they were all dry again. Then they flew down under the STAFF ONLY door once more.

Thea looked cautiously up and down the underwater tunnel, but it was still empty. With a wave of her wand and a blast of sparkling pink fairy dust, she turned Kirsty and Rachel back into girls.

She grinned at them both. "I'd better fly off to Fairyland to recharge my wand now," she said. "Then I can put a bit of sparkle back into Thursday with my Fun Day magic!" She flew over to look at Rachel's watch. "If you two hurry, you might just catch the otters being fed," she added.

"Thanks," Kirsty said. "Bye, Thea. It was great to see you again."

Thea blew them each a kiss and disappeared in a glittering pink blur. Rachel and Kirsty knew that Thea needed to give the Thursday flag to Francis, so he could run it up to the top of the Time Tower. Then Thea would stand in the middle of the clock in the Time Tower courtyard and hold up her wand. As the sun's rays

struck the shiny pattern on the Fun Day
Flag, a stream of magical sparkles would
fly toward Thea's wand and fill it with
powerful Fun Day magic.

"I hope it doesn't take Thea long to
recharge her wand," Rachel said in a
low voice as they entered the otter room.

Kirsty nodded and glanced around.
"Look at everyone in here!"

The otter room was divided in two by
a glass wall. On one side of the room
was the sea otters' exhibit, with a stream
splashing over rocks into a large pool. A
crowd of people had gathered on the
other side of the glass to watch the otters
being fed. But nobody looked very happy
about it, and even the otters looked
bored and tired. They sniffed at the small
fish that the keeper threw to them, but

they didn't seem hungry at all. Some even turned around and went back to their nests!

"Oh dear," Kirsty whispered. "Please hurry, Thea. Come and save the day! Nobody's having any fun."

The keeper frowned. "I don't know what's wrong with them," the girls heard him mutter. "Usually, these otters are the life of the party."

Just then, Rachel spotted a stream of bright pink sparkles at the back of the otters' exhibit. She nudged Kirsty. "I think Thea might

be back already," she smiled. "I'm sure I just spotted some fairy magic."

As she finished speaking, the otters suddenly seemed to wake up and shake themselves. They came tumbling into the water and splashed around merrily, chasing the fish that the keeper threw to them. Their sleek, dark heads popped up above the water then plunged under again, as soon as another fish dropped into their pool. Almost immediately, everyone in the crowd was smiling at their antics.

"They're adorable," Rachel said happily. "And look — everyone's having fun now!"

"Thea's worked her magic all right." Kirsty laughed. "Oh, and there she is!"

 The girls beamed at the tiny fairy as she peered out from behind a rock and gave them a special wave. Then she disappeared in a pink shimmer once again.

Rachel glanced down at her watch. "That was a fabulous adventure," she smiled. "And best of all, we've still got some time left before we have to meet Mom and Dad."

"So we can watch the otters and see some of the other stuff," Kirsty said.

She grinned at Rachel. "I've heard the beluga whale exhibit is worth checking out."

"Oh, yes," Rachel replied, laughing. "We definitely have to see that!"

THE FUN DAY FAIRIES

Megan, Tara, Willow, and Thea all
have their flags back. Now Rachel and
Kirsty need to help

Felicity
the Friday
Fairy!

Cooking Up a Storm

"Here's the recipe," Rachel Walker said, showing the cookbook to her best friend, Kirsty Tate. "Don't they look delicious?"

Kirsty nodded. "I love gingerbread men!" she said.

At that moment, Rachel's mom walked into the room.

"We'd better get started, girls."

"OK, Mom," Rachel agreed. She opened the fridge and Kirsty went to find the flour. Meanwhile, Mrs. Walker searched for the cookie cutter.

Mom, we don't have any eggs," Rachel called.

"And there isn't any flour in this cabinet," added Kirsty.

"That's funny," Mrs. Walker said, shaking her head. "I'm sure I saw the cookie cutter only a few days ago." She frowned. "Maybe it's up in the attic. I'll check."

Rachel sighed as her mom left the room. "This isn't any fun at all."

"You know why, don't you?" Kirsty pointed out. "It's Friday, and Felicity the Friday Fairy's flag is still missing!"